Oonga's Forest

AuthorHouse™ UK
1663 Liberty Drive
Bloomington, IN 47403 USA
www.authorhouse.co.uk
UK TFN: 0800 0148641 (Toll Free inside the UK)
UK Local: 02036 956322 (+44 20 3695 6322 from outside the UK)

This book is printed on acid-free paper.

ISBN: 978-1-6655-8549-1 (sc)
ISBN: 978-1-6655-8550-7 (e)

Print information available on the last page.

Published by AuthorHouse 05/22/2021

author HOUSE®

Oonga's Forest

Laura Findlay

In the lush green forests of Borneo lived an Orangutan called Oonga. Oonga loved her green forest that she called home.

It was full of delicious juicy fruits for her to eat

and thousands of trees for her to climb and swing from.

Out of all the trees, Oonga had a favourite. The best tree in the entire forest. It was her favourite because it was the tallest, from the top she could see the entire forest.

Green trees as far as the eye could see. It also had lots of branches.

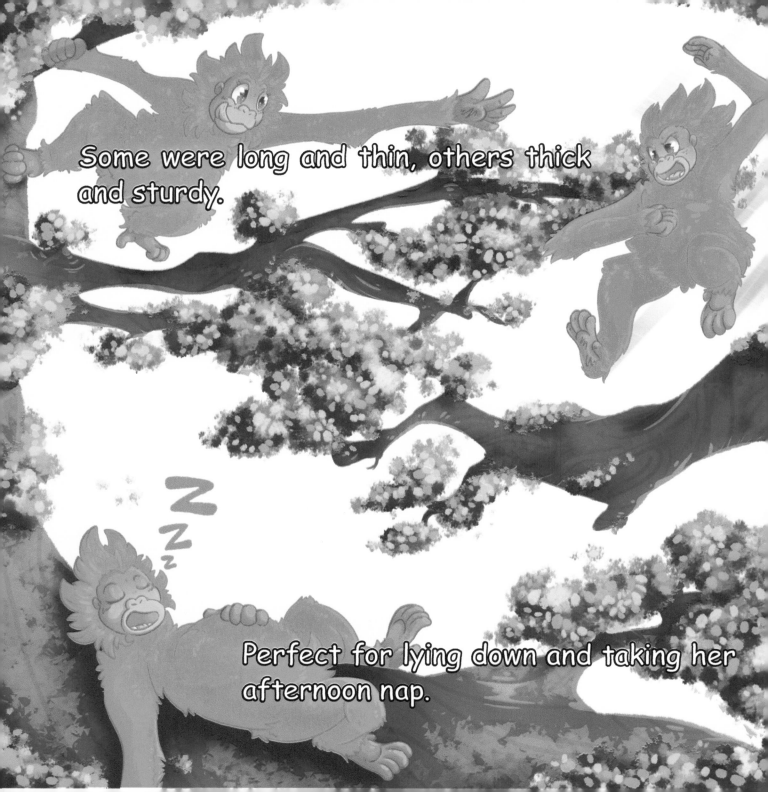

Some were long and thin, others thick and sturdy.

Perfect for lying down and taking her afternoon nap.

One day when she was having a snooze, she heard a new noise. A noise she had never heard before.

It didn't sound like her friend the tiger snoring,

and it didn't sound like her friend parrot singing his song either.

She decided to investigate.

As she got closer, the sound got louder. Oonga felt frightened. The sound was scary. It was like something big crunching through the forest. Could it be a monster?

Suddenly she saw a huge truck.

Oonga had never seen anything like it before.

With men in hard hats cutting down trees from the forest!

"What are you doing?!" She screamed.

"That is not yours! This is my home, stop!"

But the men didn't understand her, they didn't listen.

They kept chopping down tree after tree.

Oonga ran back to her friends and told them what she had saw.

A big scary machine cutting down their forest.Scary men that won't stop.

But her friends didn't believe her.

"Don't be silly Oonga", said tiger. "We have nothing to worry about. The humans won't take away all our forest. They have to leave some for us."

"Yeah", said Parrot, "humans don't need all the trees, you're worrying about nothing."

Oonga went back to her favourite tree, feeling a little better after talking to her friends.

A few days later, Oonga heard the sound again. She climbed to the top of the tallest tree and gasped.

"OH NO!" She thought, "it can't be!"

Oonga looked out over the forest. Nearly ALL the trees were gone...

Oonga started to cry. She felt a pain inside her. The place she called home, was being ripped away and she didn't understand why.

Just then, Mrs Wise the owl appeared flying on to a branch next to Oonga.

"Oonga, what is the matter?" asked Owl.

"Mrs Wise, why are the humans taking our forest away? They have their cities and homes. Why are they taking ours? I'm not knocking down their home." Sobbed Oonga.

"Oh Oonga, I understand why you're feeling so upset. Some humans are greedy, they want to take everything they can and not share it with the world.

They don't care about what it does to us animals, nature or our planet.

They don't care that what they are doing is causing so much harm to the future of the world." Explained Owl.

"That is not fair" sniffed Oonga as she wiped away her tears.

"What are we going to do when there's no forest left? Where will we go? WHAT IF THEY TAKE MY FAVOURITE TREE?!"

Owl smiled and put a wing round Oonga,

"Not all humans are like this thankfully. There are some humans out there that are trying to help us. Come with me, I can show you."

Oonga swung through the trees as she followed Owl through the forest until they reached the other side, a side of the forest that she doesn't spend much time in.

Owl pointed her wing down to the forest floor,

as Oonga looked down from a branch, she could see a group of humans.

But this time, there was no trucks cutting down trees, no humans in hard hats with clip boards. These humans were planting baby trees!

"Some humans do something called conservation. They want to save our forests, they want to save the planet, for themselves, for us and the future.

By planting more trees, it creates more homes for animals to live in and it also helps the air stay clean so that we can all breath." Said Owl.

Oonga smiled, "Wow" she said surprisingly. "This is amazing! These people really want to save the forest?"

"Yes!" said Owl. "But they need more people to help them. They can't do it all on their own. It's a big job. They can't fight the people cutting down the trees alone."

"What can we do?" asked Oonga "We can't do much," sighed Owl, "we just have to hope that the good people can do better than the people cutting down the trees and save our forest fast."

Oonga climbed down the tree to say thank you to the humans. She was welcomed with smiles and food.

"These people" thought Oonga "Are the people all humans should try to grow up to be."

Lightning Source UK Ltd.
Milton Keynes UK
UKHW052205220621
385996UK00002B/36